Miss Hubbard's New Hat

Story by **John Cunliffe**

Pictures by **Ray Mutimer**

from the original Television designs by Ivor Wood

Hippo Books
Scholastic Children's Books
London

Scholastic Children's Books,
Scholastic Publications Ltd,
7-9 Pratt Street, London NW1 0AE, UK

Scholastic Inc.,
730 Broadway, New York, NY 10003, USA

Scholastic Canada Ltd,
123 Newkirk Road, Richmond Hill,
Ontario, Canada L4C 3G5

Ashton Scholastic Pty Ltd,
PO Box 579, Gosford, New South Wales,
Australia

Ashton Scholastic Ltd,
Private Bag 1, Penrose, Auckland,
New Zealand

First published by André Deutsch Ltd, 1991
First published in paperback by Scholastic Publications Ltd, 1992

Text copyright © John Cunliffe
Illustrations copyright © André Deutsch Ltd, Scholastic Publications Ltd,
and Woodland Animations Ltd

ISBN 0 590 55015 2

Typeset by AKM Associates (UK) Ltd, Southall, London
Printed in Belgium by Proost International Bookproduction
All rights reserved.

10 9 8 7 6 5 4 3

Miss Hubbard got up early on Thursday morning. It was the first Thursday in the month, and that was the day for delivering the *Parish News* for the Reverend Timms. She oiled her bike, and put both baskets on, front and back. She put on her blue coat. She looked in the mirror.

"Now," she said, "which hat shall I wear?"

She put on her usual brown hat.

"Hmmmm . . ." she said. "It doesn't look right. Let's see. What about the new one?"

Miss Hubbard had a new hat. A blue hat. But she hadn't been out in it yet. She tried it on now.

"Hmmmmm . . ." she said. "It's a bit plain; but it makes a change."

So she kept it on.

Off she went, on her bike.

She called at the church for the *Parish News*.

"Oh! bless me!" said the Reverend Timms. "It's you, Miss Hubbard!"

"Who did you think it was, Reverend?"

"I saw your head, coming along above the hedge, with a lovely blue hat on, and . . . well, I didn't know *who* it was."

Miss Hubbard looked in the vestry mirror.

"It is a nice colour," she said, "but it's rather plain.

It needs a little . . ."

"Adornment?"

"Quite so, Reverend."

"Here's a sprig of holly, left over from Christmas.

How about that?"

"Lovely! A nice spot of colour. Thank you,

Reverend."

Miss Hubbard tucked the holly into the band of her

hat. Then she filled up the baskets of her bike, front

and back, with copies of the *Parish News*, and away

she went.

Miss Hubbard called at Thompson Ground.

"Morning!" she called. "*Parish News*! Read all about it!"

Dorothy Thompson came out, with her egg-basket.

"And a good morning to you, Miss Hubbard. Ooh! I like your hat. It's a lovely colour. But . . ."

"I know. Needs a little decoration?"

"That's it. Decoration," said Dorothy, looking at the hens, as they clucked and pecked about the yard.

"Feathers, now; they're pretty."

"Just the thing," said Miss Hubbard. "Look at that one!"

A speckled hen went by. It had lovely long silky feathers, speckled in black, and brown, and white. When Miss Hubbard pointed, it ran for its life.

"Oh, chucky chucky, we'll not pull your feathers out,"

said Dorothy, "but you might just have dropped one for Miss Hubbard's hat?"

They followed the hen to her home. There, by her roost, was a lovely long feather.

"And a speckled egg as well," said Dorothy, "for your tea."

"Delightful!" said Miss Hubbard. "Just the thing.
Thank you very much. And thanks to chucky."
She tucked the feather into her hat.
"Very stylish," said Dorothy.
Miss Hubbard popped the egg into her handbag.
Then she went on her way, with the feather waving in
the breeze.

Miss Hubbard called at Greendale Farm.

"Morning!" she called. "*Parish News*! Read all about it!"

"And a very good morning to you," said Mrs Pottage. "And what a lovely new hat you've got on. Really stylish, with that feather."

"Hello, Miss Hubbard," said Katy. "Would you like a chocolate?"

"That's a nice hat," said Tom.

"Thank you," said Miss Hubbard, to them all.

"Just a small one, then. What a lovely ribbon!"

There was a silky red ribbon on the box of chocolates.

"It would look nice on your hat," said Katy.

She took it off the chocolate-box, and held it up to

Miss Hubbard's hat.

"My favourite colour," said Miss Hubbard.

"May I?"

"Oooh, yes!" said Katy. "Do! It's just right."

Miss Hubbard fitted the red ribbon round her hat.

"It sets it off a treat," she said. "I'd better be off,

now. Thanks everyone! Bye!"

And Miss Hubbard was on her way.

Miss Hubbard called on Granny Dryden.

"Good morning!" she called. "*Parish News*! Read all about it!"

"That's a nice hat," said Granny Dryden. "I like the feather. My old mother once had one like that. She went to the Jubilee in it. Now where are my glasses?"

"Glad you like it, Mrs Dryden. Would you like to borrow mine?"

Granny Dryden put on Miss Hubbard's glasses to look at the *Parish News*, whilst Miss Hubbard sat down with a cup of tea.

"It just needs something to finish it off," said Granny Dryden.

"The *Parish News*?"

"No, your hat. Now my mother used to have a bunch of cherries made of felt. I might still have them somewhere. Sit still and finish your tea and I'll just have a look."

Miss Hubbard sighed. Oh, dear! She didn't really want felt cherries on her hat. It would be just too much. But she would have to take them, to please Granny Dryden. Perhaps she wouldn't find them? But she did. She soon came back, holding them up with a smile.

"Here we are! Just the thing."

Granny Dryden brought her needle-and-thread and sewed the cherries on to the front of Miss Hubbard's hat-band. They wobbled about when she moved, and she went cross-eyed with looking at them.

"Thank you, Mrs Dryden," said Miss Hubbard.

"I must be on my way. Good-bye!"

But Miss Hubbard could not ride her bike with felt cherries bobbling about in front of her eyes. As soon as she was round the corner, she stopped and took her hat off. She began picking at the stitches that held the cherries. Just then, Peter Fogg came by with his tractor and trailer. Miss Hubbard waved to him to stop.

"Hi! Peter! Stop! *Parish News*! Read all about it!"

"Thanks," said Peter.

Then Peter began to sing a song to Miss Hubbard.

"Where did you get that hat?

Where did you get it from?

Where did you get that hat ? . . ."

"That's enough!" said Miss Hubbard. "I'm in no mood for funny songs. It was a nice plain hat at breakfast-time. You don't happen to have a pair of scissors in your pocket, do you, Peter?"

"I might have some, somewhere," said Peter, grinning. "Sorry, Miss Hubbard. It's only a song my old dad sings. It *is* a nice hat, really."

He went to look in his tool-box, to see if he had anything that would unpick Granny Dryden's strong stitches.

Dr Gilbertson came along, and stopped to have chat with Miss Hubbard. Miss Hubbard put her hat down on the back of Peter's trailer, to give the doctor a copy of the *Parish News*. Then Dr Gilbertson said, "And how's your backache these days?"

Miss Hubbard was so busy telling the doctor about her sore back, and how it had got better since her holiday in Spain, that she forgot her hat for the moment. When Peter called, from his tractor, "Sorry, Miss Hubbard. I haven't got any scissors. I'd best be on my way. Ted will be waiting with the next load of manure." Miss Hubbard just gave him a wave, and went on talking to Dr Gilbertson.

". . . and so my back's been fine ever since," she said.
"But what are you doing without a hat, today?" said
Dr Gilbertson. "I've never seen you without a hat
before."

"I've got my new blue hat," said Miss Hubbard.
"Look . . ."

She turned to see where it was, then saw that it was
gone.

"Oh . . . ?" said Miss Hubbard. "Where has it gone?
Goodness, me, I must have put it down on Peter's
trailer when I got out your *Parish News*! Hi! Peter!
Come back!"

But he was too far away to hear her above the roar of the tractor.

"Didn't he say something about manure?" said Dr Gilbertson.

"He *did*," said Miss Hubbard. "And if Ted doesn't look where he's tipping it . . ."

"Couldn't you catch him on your bike?" said Dr Gilbertson.

"Not up that hill," said Miss Hubbard.

Just then, there was a *toot-toot* behind them.
Who should it be, but Postman Pat in his red van.
"Just the man," said Miss Hubbard.
"Morning!" said Pat, as he stopped. "I have some
letters for both of you today. There's something
different about you, Miss Hubbard, and I can't think
what it is!"

"Never mind that," said Miss Hubbard, popping the
letters in her basket, "follow that tractor. Peter's gone
off with my hat on his trailer."

"That's what it is," said Pat. "No hat."

"Hurry up, man!" said Miss Hubbard.

By now, Peter was no more than a dot on the far
hillside.

"Your hat won't come to any harm on Peter's trailer," said Pat. "Unless he's gone to see Mrs Bagenal, and her goats take a fancy to it."

"No," said Miss Hubbard, "he's loading manure, with Ted. If I know Ted, he'll dump a load of manure on top of my hat without even seeing it. Hurry up! Oh, Pat, please do hurry!"

"That's different," said Pat. "I have a letter for him, anyway. It'll be urgent delivery, now. Off we go! Hold your whiskers, Jess."

Pat jumped into his van, and whizzed away, after Peter.

Pat was just in time. Ted was backing the other tractor up, with a full load of lovely fresh manure, ready to tip it on to Peter's trailer, right on top of Miss Hubbard's hat.

"Stop!" shouted Pat. "Stop!"

"What's up?" said Ted.

"Urgent delivery," said Pat, snatching the hat out of harm's way.

"Oh!" said Peter. "That's Miss Hubbard's hat. How did it get there?"

Pat told him.

"I'll nip back to her with it," he said. "She was a bit worried in case you manured it."

Pat put the hat on the seat, by Jess, to take it back to Miss Hubbard. Jess thought the cherries looked tasty. He pulled them off, when Pat wasn't looking, and gave them a nibble. He spat them out when he found they were made of felt.

"Naughty, Jess," said Pat, when he saw the cherries.
But Miss Hubbard was pleased when she saw what
Jess had done.

"Good cat," she said, and Jess purred. "Have a
Parish News, Pat."

"Thanks," said Pat. "Cheerio!"

"Bye, Pat!"

Miss Hubbard put her blue hat firmly on her head, and cycled away. There were still a lot of copies of the *Parish News* to be delivered.